North America

Mary Kate Bolinder

Consultants

Andrea Johnson, Ph.D.
Assistant Professor of History
California State University, Dominguez Hills

Esperanza Noriega
General Director
New Edulight, Mexico

Jon Anger
English, History, and ELD Teacher
Novato Unified School District

Publishing Credits

Rachelle Cracchiolo, M.S.Ed., *Publisher*
Emily R. Smith, M.A.Ed., *SVP of Content Development*
Véronique Bos, *Vice President of Creative*
Dani Neiley, *Editor*
Fabiola Sepulveda, *Series Graphic Designer*

Image Credits: p.10 (top) Bridgeman Images/Peter Newark Western Americana; p.11 (top) Getty Images/Giles Clarke; p.11 (bottom) Alamy/Reuters; p.12 (top) Getty Images/Bloomberg; p.13 (top) Bridgeman Images/Stefano Bianchetti; p.14 Getty Images/DEA Dea Dagliorti; p.15 (top) Associated Press; p.16 (left) Archivo General de la Nación Mexico; all other images from iStock and/or Shutterstock

Library of Congress Cataloging-in-Publication Data

Names: Bolinder, Mary Kate, author.
Title: North America / Mary Kate Bolinder.
Description: Huntington Beach, CA : Teacher Created Materials, Inc, [2023] | Includes index. | Audience: Ages 8-18 | Summary: "Welcome to North America! It is the third largest continent in the world. Come along as we explore its history and geography. You'll encounter wild animals and dazzling landscapes. This book is a celebration of all the things that make North America great"-- Provided by publisher.
Identifiers: LCCN 2022038212 (print) | LCCN 2022038213 (ebook) | ISBN 9781087695099 (paperback) | ISBN 9781087695259 (ebook)
Subjects: LCSH: North America--Juvenile literature.
Classification: LCC E40.5 .B65 2023 (print) | LCC E40.5 (ebook) | DDC 970--dc23/eng/20211220
LC record available at https://lccn.loc.gov/2022038212
LC ebook record available at https://lccn.loc.gov/2022038213

Shown on the cover is Yoho National Park in Canada.

This book may not be reproduced or distributed in any way without prior written consent from the publisher.

5482 Argosy Avenue
Huntington Beach, CA 92649
www.tcmpub.com
ISBN 978-1-0876-9509-9
© 2023 Teacher Created Materials, Inc.

Havana, Cuba

Table of Contents

Welcome to North America 4
Geography through Time 6
North American History 10
Government Structure 16
Trade, Resources, and Tourism 20
North America Today 26
Map It! 28
Glossary 30
Index 31
Learn More! 32

Welcome to North America

North America is the third-largest **continent**. It lies between the Atlantic and Pacific Oceans. The continent begins near the North Pole. It stretches south almost to the **equator**. On this continent, there is a wide range of climates. The geography is varied, too. There are forests, mountains, and plains. There are scorching hot deserts and icy **tundras**.

Three large countries exist in North America. They are Canada, the United States, and Mexico. Seven small countries south of Mexico are also part of North America. These countries are known as Central America. There are also many islands in the Caribbean Sea. They are also part of North America. This is true for Greenland, too.

Indigenous peoples have lived on the land for thousands of years. The land and the people here have changed through time. Today, many diverse groups of people call North America home. And people from all over the world come to visit and live in North America.

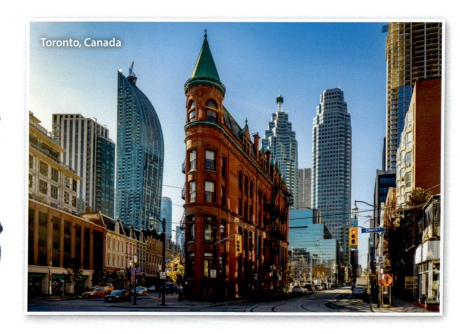

Toronto, Canada

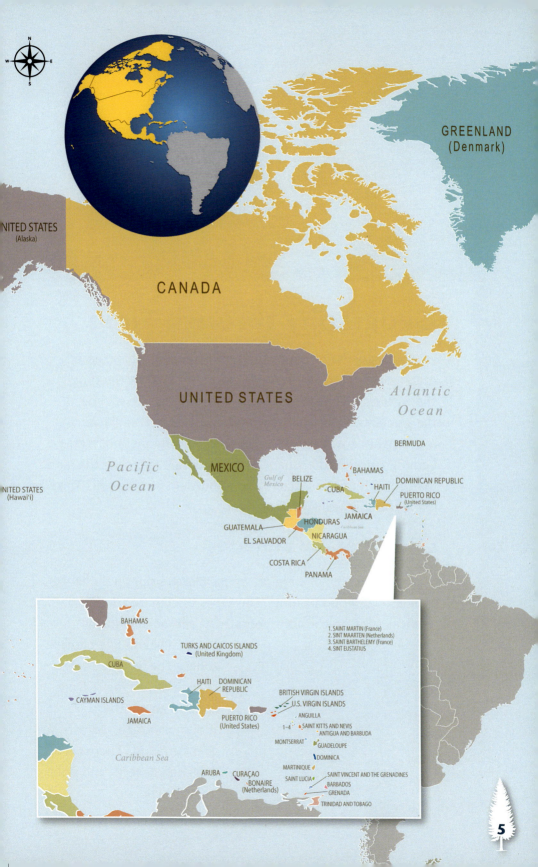

Glacier Bay National Park in Alaska

Geography through Time

Long ago, the plates of the earth collided. This created mountains on the North American continent. At the time, the whole continent was covered in **glaciers**. Over time, the glaciers began to slowly melt and move. This glacier movement caused **erosion** that formed canyons and river beds. Erosion further shaped the mountain ranges of the land. Melted water from glaciers added nutrients to the soil. This made the soil healthy for plants to grow.

Land of Many Climates

A climate zone is a region whose climate does not change over a long period of time. The types of climate zones are tropical, subtropical, continental, dry, and polar. North America has all five climate zones. The land and **terrain** change as you move from zone to zone. There are mountain ranges, forests, and farmland. There are beaches, deserts, and polar regions, too.

Taboga Island, Panama

Canada

Canada is the largest country in North America. Canada has more lakes than any other country in the world. It also has the longest coastline in the world. Icebergs can be seen in parts of northern Canada. There are many other geographic features in Canada. More than 40 percent of the country is forest. **Temperate** rain forests are on the east coast. They have a mild climate but also receive heavy rainfall.

Canadian rain forest

These rocks are part of the Canadian Shield.

Rock On!

At the northernmost part of Canada is an area called the *Canadian Shield*. A shield is an area of exposed ancient rocks. Some of the oldest rocks in the world can be found in shields. Scientists estimate parts of these rocks are more than four billion years old. This rocky area extends into Greenland.

The United States

The United States is in the middle of North America. It has a mix of terrain, including mountain ranges, deserts, and plains. The Rocky Mountains in the West and the Appalachian Mountains in the East both run all the way into Canada. In between these ranges are the Great Plains and the Midwest. Much of these regions has been turned into rich farmland that helps feed the country. Most of the country has a temperate climate. Its weather changes with the seasons.

Bison graze in the grassland of Custer State Park, South Dakota.

Sonoran Desert

Mexico

Mountain ranges and deserts cover much of Mexico. The Sonoran Desert in the North reaches into the United States. Saguaro cacti grow in this region. These desert plants can grow to over 40 feet (12 meters) tall. Some of them are more than 100 years old. The Sierra Madre in the West is Mexico's largest mountain range. But the country is not all mountains and deserts. The state of Chiapas has a tropical rain forest. Many types of wildlife, such as jaguars, toucans, and iguanas, live there.

Bodies of Water

There are no landlocked countries in North America. Every country borders a large body of water. Many bodies of water in North America border multiple countries. Canada and the United States share the Great Lakes. The Gulf of Mexico borders Mexico, the United States, and the northern part of the Caribbean. The Caribbean Sea borders the Caribbean and part of Central America.

Go, Go, Archipelago!

The Caribbean Sea is dotted with hundreds of islands. A large chain of islands is called an *archipelago*. The islands in the Caribbean are popular tourist destinations. They have  beautiful blue water, sandy beaches, and warm weather. However, these islands face many storms during the rainy seasons. The humid air and tropical waters can cause hurricanes.

North American History

Indigenous peoples have lived in North America for thousands of years. Researchers used to have a theory about the first people to live on the continent. They thought the people used a land bridge thousands of years ago. Researchers thought the bridge started in Siberia, a region of northern Asia. The people were thought to have crossed from Asia to current-day Alaska. Today, this idea is being challenged. Some researchers think the first people may have arrived by using an ice bridge from Europe to North America. Or the first voyagers may have used boats to get there. Whatever way they arrived, Indigenous peoples moved in groups and spread throughout the continent. They were the first to call North America home.

painting of a Lakota village

This museum guide teaches visitors about Tlingit heritage in Haines, Alaska.

Inuit, Métis, and First Nations leaders with a Canadian politician

First Nations

Most Indigenous peoples in Canada are known as First Nations. Inuit and Métis are also native groups there. Today, more than one million people in Canada identify as part of one of these groups.

In the past, First Nations peoples in Canada relied on the land for survival. Those who lived along the Atlantic and Pacific coasts were skilled at hunting and fishing. They fished for salmon in the Pacific. Cod was found in the Atlantic. They hunted large animals, including moose, bears, and caribou. They also were skilled trappers. They trapped small animals, such as beavers and rabbits. The animals had valuable **pelts**. These could be traded and exchanged for other goods. Animal fur provided warmth all year.

Water Protectors

Members of the Anishinabek Nation live around the northern borders of the Great Lakes in Canada. The Anishinabek Nation has a strong connection to water. Autumn Peltier is a young Anishinaabe activist. She speaks up to protect native waters from pollution.

Indigenous Peoples of Mexico

Many Indigenous peoples lived (and still live) in Mexico. The Aztecs were located in central and southern Mexico. They built complex cities and created a calendar system. The Aztec Empire was at its height in the 15th and 16th centuries. The Zapotec and Mixtec peoples lived in southern Mexico. The Zapotec were farmers and grew most of their food. The Mixtec were also farmers. Today, many Mixtec and Zapotec peoples go to northern Mexico for work. San Quintín and Mexicali in Baja California have many jobs in agriculture.

Northern Mexico is home to many Indigenous peoples. One notable group is the Yaqui. Today, they mainly live in Sonora, Sinaloa, and Arizona. Over time, they have fought many battles to keep their land. They have also fought to keep their water supply safe.

Zapotec women create pottery in Oaxaca, Mexico.

Zapotec and Mixtec peoples used to live in the city of Monte Albán in Oaxaca, Mexico.

Wampanoag leader Massasoit meets with colonists at Plymouth in the 1620s.

American Indians

In the United States, American Indians live in groups known as tribes, nations, or bands. In the past, some nations, such as the Navajo, were **nomadic.** They traveled around the land in search of food. Hunting and fishing were common, and they also gathered plants to eat. Other tribes on the East Coast stayed in one place. This was true for some Wampanoag tribes. For food, they grew their own crops and gathered wild rice. Salmon and shellfish were caught in the rivers. In their villages, they built wigwams, or longhouses.

Mesa Verde

Many American Indian sites are preserved throughout the United States. This may include homes or buildings. One site is Mesa Verde in Colorado. The Ancestral Pueblo peoples lived there. They built their homes into the side of a cliff. People can visit and learn about the cliff dwellings today.

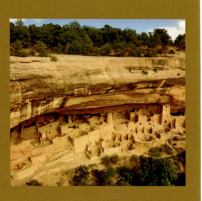

Immigration

European **immigrants** first came to North America in the 1600s. They came for new opportunities and freedom. People continued to come to North America over time. In the early 1900s, the United States saw a boom in immigration. Immigrants from around the world came to the United States on ships.

Most of them settled in cities. But it was not easy for them to get started in new places. They had to find jobs and places to live. Some children could not go to school. Instead, they had to work. Many people worked on farms and in factories. These jobs were hard. They involved a lot of physical labor.

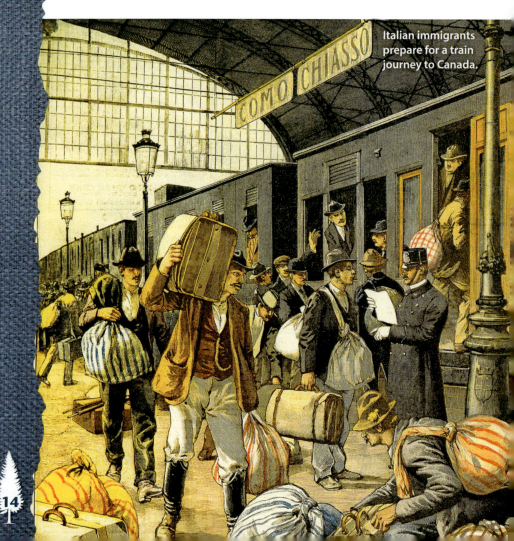

Italian immigrants prepare for a train journey to Canada.

Languages

People from all over the world live in North America. In the United States, hundreds of languages are spoken. Because of this, the United States does not have an official language. In Mexico, the official language is Spanish. This is true for some countries in Central America, too. Canada's official languages are French and English. In the Caribbean, six official languages are spoken. And across North America, hundreds of Indigenous languages are spoken.

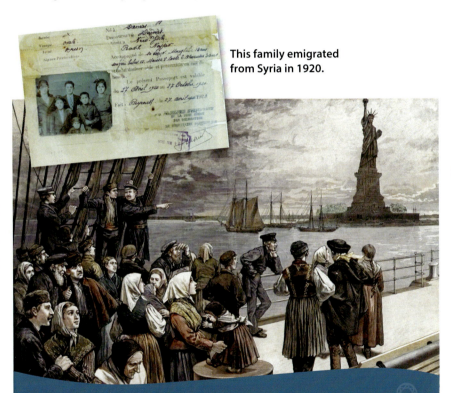

This family emigrated from Syria in 1920.

New Life in a New Land

From 1900 to 1915, more than 15 million immigrants came to the United States. Most of them came from Europe. They entered the United States through Ellis Island in New York. They went past the Statue of Liberty in New York Harbor. The statue's raised torch is meant as a symbol of enlightenment. It represents the path to liberty, or freedom.

Government Structure

In the 1770s, people in **colonial** America wanted change. They did not want to be controlled by Great Britain. So, a group of men came together to write a document. It is called the Declaration of Independence. It tells of their desire to be free from British rule. After writing it, the colonies went to war with Britain. They won their independence.

These colonies became known as the United States. This was the first country to write a declaration of independence. But the United States still needed a plan for its government. In 1787, the U.S. Constitution was completed. A constitution tells how a government is set up. It lists the powers of the government. It gives the laws of the country. It outlines the rights of the people who live there. All the other countries in North America also have constitutions.

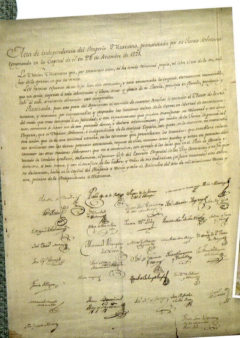

Mexico's Declaration of Independence

Benjamin Franklin, John Adams, and Thomas Jefferson review a draft of the Declaration of Independence.

Independence Day parade in Mexico City, Mexico

Each country in North America has its own way of organizing land. In Canada, land is split into **provinces**. Canada has 10 provinces. Costa Rica and Panama have provinces, too. Belize has districts. In the rest of the Central American countries, land is split into departments. In the United States and Mexico, areas are known as states. Mexico has 32 states. The United States has 50 states. Each province, district, deparment, or state has its own capital city. Each one has its own local governments, too.

Young People in Action

Young people can make a difference in their governments. Citizens in Mexico, the United States, and Canada can vote at the age of 18. Anyone can participate in protests and rally for issues they care about. They can call and write to their leaders to make their voices heard.

Government Leaders

The U.S. and Mexican governments are both **democracies**. In a democracy, the people of the country vote for their leaders. There are elections for local and state government leaders. Elections are held for national government leaders, too. Both Mexico and the United States elect presidents. The president's job is to lead the country.

In Mexico, the Congress of the Union makes laws. It is made up of two branches. The first is the Senate of the Republic. The second is the Chamber of Deputies.

Andrés Manuel López Obrador, Mexico's 65th president

Mexico's National Palace in Mexico City

Canada's Parliament in Ottawa

Justin Trudeau, Canada's 23rd prime minister

In the United States, Congress makes laws. Congress has two branches. They are the Senate and the House of Representatives.

Canada's government is a constitutional monarchy. This means Canada's government includes a monarch. A monarch is a ruler, such as a king or a queen. The monarch of the United Kingdom is also the monarch of Canada. But the monarch does not have the power to make laws. Instead, that is up to the local Canadian leaders. The people of Canada elect a leader called a prime minister. The Parliament of Canada makes laws. It has two branches. They are the Senate and House of Commons.

Most countries in Central America are republics. This means citizens vote to elect representatives in government. This is similar to how people in the United States and Mexico elect leaders. Belize has a constitutional monarchy like Canada.

Presidential Term Limits

The United States has a presidential election every four years. A person can only be elected twice. Guatemala and Honduras also have elections every four years. But a person can only be elected president once. In Mexico, elections are held every six years. A person can only be elected once. In Nicaragua, elections are held every five years. A person can be elected president multiple times.

Tourists can view Niagara Falls from both the United States and Canada.

Trade, Resources, and Tourism

North America has many valuable **natural resources**. North American countries ship their goods around the world. But they do most of their trading with one another. Mexico, the United States, and Canada have a trade agreement. This makes it easier to get the goods and services they need the most.

Where Two Oceans Meet

The Panama Canal was built to connect shipping trade routes from the Atlantic Ocean to the Pacific Ocean. The Panama Canal is about 50 miles (80 kilometers) long. It took 10 years to build. It allows goods to be shipped more quickly.

Natural Resources

North America has many energy resources. Coal, natural gas, and oil are major **exports**. The United States produces a lot of gas and oil. Most of it is exported to Canada and Mexico. The United States also has lots of iron ore, copper, and zinc. These resources are used in cars and electronics. Factories in Canada, the United States, and Mexico make cars and car parts.

Many precious metals and minerals are mined in North America. In 1848, gold was discovered in California, sparking a gold rush. Today, most U.S. gold is exported from Nevada. Mexico produces more silver than any other country.

Forests cover much of the land in Canada. Some forested areas are actually tree farms. The trees are cut down, and more are planted. The cut trees are turned into lumber. The lumber is shipped around the world. Wood is used as an important building material.

oil pumps in North Dakota

Farming

There is a lot of farmland in North America. Food grown on the continent is exported around the world. Some of the world's wheat comes from the Great Plains in the United States. One of the largest exports from North America is corn. Corn, or maize, was a staple food for Indigenous peoples in North America. Today, people around the world enjoy food made from corn, such as cereal, tortillas, and popcorn. Farmers also grow corn to feed livestock.

Tropical fruits grow in Central America and the Caribbean. Fruits, such as oranges, bananas, and avocados, are grown and harvested. Farmers grow sugarcane, cocoa, and coffee beans there, too.

A farmer plants corn in Tabasco, Mexico.

Banff National Park, Canada

Protecting the Land

As the population of North America grew, more cities and towns were built. More farms were built, and more resources were extracted. But some people saw a need for protecting certain areas. They created national parks. These are special places in a country that cannot be changed. The water, plants, wildlife, and soil are preserved. This helps protect the environment. It also protects resources for future generations. National parks can be found across North America. In the United States, you can visit trees that are thousands of years old. You can visit deserts and forests. In Canada, many national parks have stunning lakes and mountains. Mexico's parks include canyons, reefs, and even Maya ruins.

Yellowstone

In 1872, the first ever national park was created. Yellowstone National Park in the United States is filled with forests, canyons, rivers, and geysers. A geyser is a hot spring of water that erupts. The park's most well-known geyser is Old Faithful. Its eruptions happen frequently and are easy to predict.

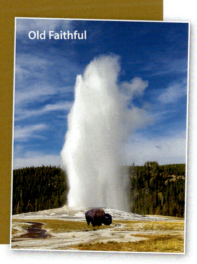

Old Faithful

23

Tourism

People come from all over the world to visit North America. Each country has many historical sites and large cities. The Caribbean is a popular place to visit. It has a tropical climate and beautiful beaches. Many people in the Caribbean work in **tourism**. They work in hotels and restaurants. Some of them work as local travel guides. Mexico City has many famous museums. There are also famous churches and parks. One of the biggest tourist sites in the world is in the United States. It's Disney World in Florida, and it has four theme parks and two water parks.

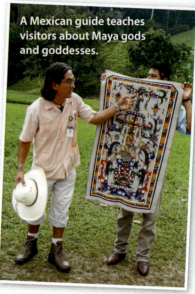

A Mexican guide teaches visitors about Maya gods and goddesses.

Maya temple in Yucatán, Mexico

Street festivals are popular tourist attractions in North America. People eat local food and listen to music. There are costumes and parades, too. Carnival is celebrated in some countries in Central America and the Caribbean. Public celebrations are held in February and early March. Carnival is also celebrated in some states in Mexico. Mardi Gras is another street festival. A big celebration is held every year in Louisiana. Some celebrations are held in Alabama, Florida, and Texas, too.

Mardi Gras parade in New Orleans, Louisiana

Technology

North America is known around the world for its technology companies. Apple® and Google™ started in California in the United States. Canada and Mexico are seeing growth in these jobs. The COVID-19 pandemic caused a boom in this industry. More people stayed at home in 2020, so they relied on online services more than usual. Technology is constantly advancing. New products and inventions are being made every day.

Industries in Greenland

Greenland's main industry is fishing. The water surrounding it is full of fish and crustaceans, such as shrimp. Agriculture is not very common in Greenland. This is because ice covers roughly 80 percent of the land. But some crops, including hay and vegetables, are grown. Tourism has also been a rising industry in recent years. More people from overseas are interested in visiting Greenland.

North America Today

More than 600 million people call North America home. And millions of people visit North America every year. People from all over the world come to see the many features of the land. There are crystal blue seas in the Caribbean. Huge mountain ranges can be seen across the continent. There are plains, deserts, and even rain forests. Nearly every type of landform can be found.

North America is a place rich in history and culture. Many historical sites in these countries tell the stories of the past. Museums help tell these stories, too. Ruins show what life was like long ago. Indigenous peoples today continue their traditions in their communities. And immigrants continue to come to North America to begin new lives.

Mexican dancers perform at a festival in Yucatán.

Québec City, Canada

Technology made in North America is part of daily life for people everywhere. It helps people communicate around the world. Many other resources and goods are exported from North America.

People have lived in North America for thousands of years. North America will continue to grow and change as time goes on. What changes do you think will happen in the coming years?

Growing Every Day

The population of the United States is the third largest in the world. It has more than 320 million people. Mexico has more than 128 million. Canada has more than 38 million. Those numbers may seem big. But two countries have larger populations. They are China and India. Their populations each have more than 1 billion people!

New York City

Map It!

It's time to hit the road on a national park road trip! Pick a country in North America. Plan a trip to at least five national parks in the country.

1. Draw or trace an outline of the country you chose on a sheet of paper or poster board, or print a blank copy of the country's map.

2. Research the national parks in this country. Choose five of them, and mark them on your map with a small drawing for each. (For example, if you want to travel to Banff National Park in Canada, draw a mountain peak or a lake.)

3. Create a map key to label the parks you've chosen.

4. Make a list of two to three important landmarks in each park. Write these on the side or back of your map.

5. Plan the route you will take across the country, and trace it on your map.

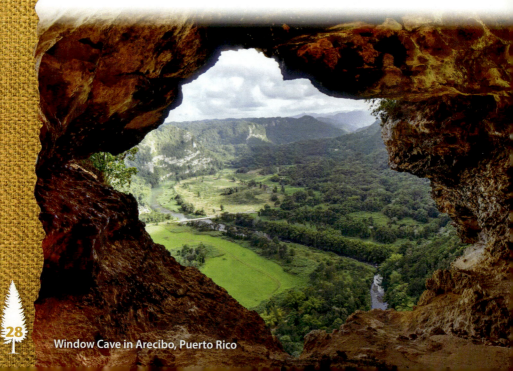

Window Cave in Arecibo, Puerto Rico

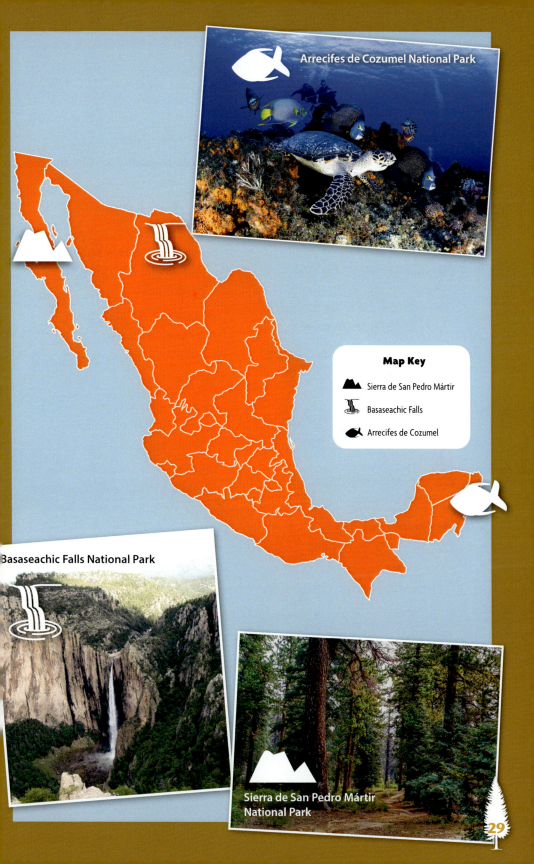

Glossary

colonial—of or relating to the original 13 colonies that formed the United States

continent—one of the seven large groups of land on Earth

democracies—governments in which people choose leaders by voting

equator—an imaginary circle drawn around Earth that is equally distant from the north pole and the south pole

erosion—the process of wearing away land by natural forces, such as ice or water

exports—products that are sent to another state or country to be sold there

glaciers—slow-moving masses or rivers of ice

immigrants—people who come to a country to live there

natural resources—materials supplied by nature that can be used by humans

nomadic—roaming from place to place frequently

pelts—animal skins with fur or wool

provinces—regions of a country that have their own local governments

temperate—relating to an area or climate with mild temperatures

terrain—land

tourism—the activity of traveling to a place for pleasure

tundras—flat areas of land where the soil is always frozen and short plants grow; treeless regions of mountainous land above timberlines

Grand Cayman Island in the Caribbean

Index

Atlantic Ocean, 4–5, 11, 20

Aztec, 12

Baja California, 12

Belize, 5, 17, 19

Canada, 4–5, 7–9, 11, 14–15, 17, 19–21, 23, 25–27

Caribbean, 4–5, 9, 15, 22, 24–26

Central America, 4, 9, 15, 17, 19, 22, 25

Europe, 14–15

First Nations, 11

Greenland, 4–5, 7, 25

Guatemala, 5, 19

Honduras, 5, 19

Indigenous peoples, 4, 10–12, 22, 26

Inuit, 11, 13

Maya, 23–24

Mesa Verde, 13

Métis, 11

Mexico, 4–5, 9, 12, 15, 17–27

Mixtec, 12

national parks, 23

Navajo, 13

New York, 15, 27

Niagara Falls, 9, 20–21

Nicaragua, 5, 17, 19

Pacific Ocean, 4–5, 11, 20

Panama Canal, 20

United States, 4–5, 8–9, 13–25, 27

Wampanoag, 13

Zapotec, 12

Learn More!

John Muir was a Scottish immigrant to the United States. He loved nature and helped establish some national parks. He once walked from the midwestern United States all the way to the Gulf of Mexico. He kept a nature journal on his walk and called it *A Thousand-Mile Walk to the Gulf*. You may not walk as far as Muir, but you can still make a nature journal of your own!

- Research a national park trail. Imagine you are hiking that trail. Or, you can research a hiking or walking trail in your community and go there.
- Create your own nature journal entry, just like Muir once did.
- Record important facts about your walk. This may include what animals you can see, what plants and trees are growing, the weather, and any interesting geographic features.
- Sketch or glue photos of what you can see in your journal.

Yosemite National Park, California